SIBLEY

AND THE

NIGHT NOISES

BUMP! CREAK

GLUMP! SCRUNCH

PITTER PATTER WHUMP!

Written and Illustrated by

Dr. Kimberly Brayman

For information regarding permission please write to:
Dr. Kimberly Brayman: info@KimberlyBraymanAuthor.com

For bulk and wholesale orders please email Dr. Kimberly Brayman: info@KimberlyBraymanAuthor.com

ISBN: 978-1-951688-23-3 (paperback)

Written and Illustrated by: Dr. Kimberly Brayman

First Edition

Team Published with Artistic Warrior
artisticwarrior.com

Dedicated to all those who
struggle with a peaceful night's sleep.

Pediatric studies estimate that sleep problems affect 25-50% of children and 40% of all teens.

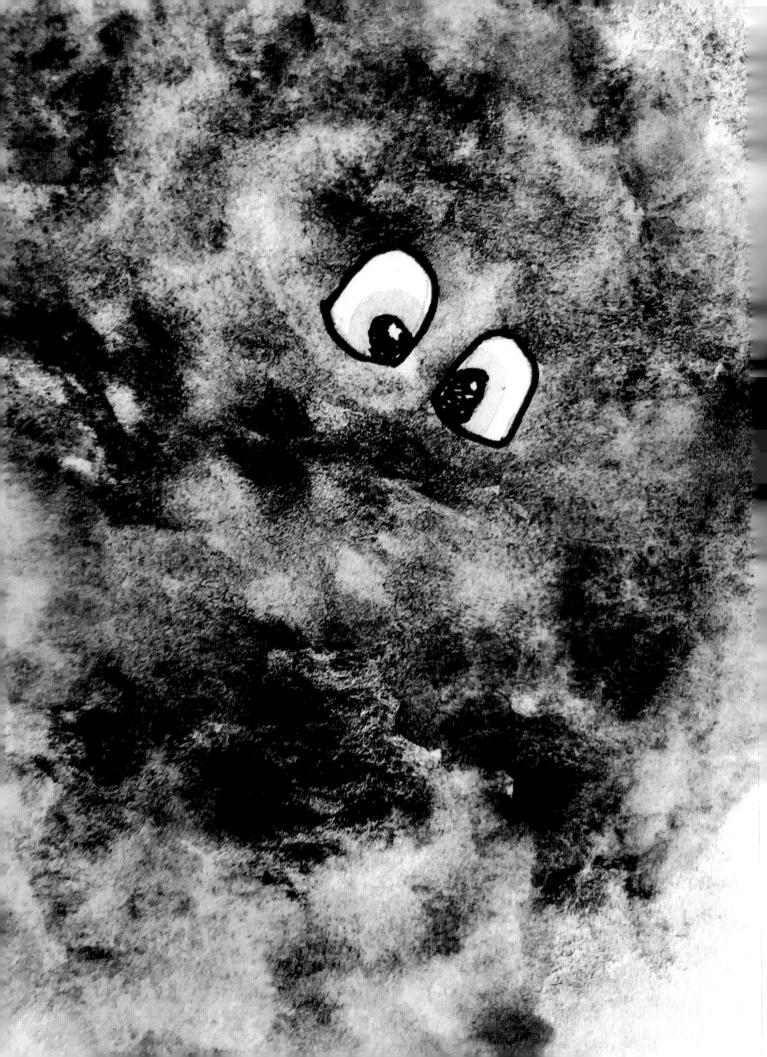

Sibley woke.
It was nighttime
and she was scared.

"I'm okay.
I'm okay.
I'm okay,"
she said.

But she didn't feel okay.
She felt jiggly,
wiggly, and
squiggly
in her belly.

Sibley sat up.
She scrunched up her legs and
wrapped her arms around her knees.
Her toes stuck out
from her pajama bottoms.
She scrunched them up too.

Sibley pulled the bedcovers
all the way over her head.

"I'm okay.
I'm okay.
I'm okay,"
she said.

But she didn't feel okay.
She felt jiggly,
wiggly, and
squiggly
in her belly.

Sibley jumped so high that her whole body
and all the covers flew up in the air.

When she landed,
the covers fluttered down around her.

"I'm okay.
I'm okay.
I'm okay,"
she said.

But she didn't feel okay.
She felt jiggly,
wiggly, and
squiggly
in her belly.

WHUMP!

WHUMP!

Sibley gasped, grabbed her
emergency flashlight, and turned it on. Something jumped out of the
dark and landed on her bedcovers.
It was inches away.

"I'm okay.
I'm okay.
I'm okay,"
she said.

But she didn't feel okay.
She felt jiggly,
wiggly, and
squiggly
in her belly.

FOOO-UMP!
FOOO-UMP!

Sibley's mouth opened wide.
Something slid down her bedcovers
and landed beside her on the bed.

"I'm okay.
I'm okay.
I'm okay,"
she said.

But she didn't feel okay.
She felt jiggly,
wiggly, and
squiggly in her belly.

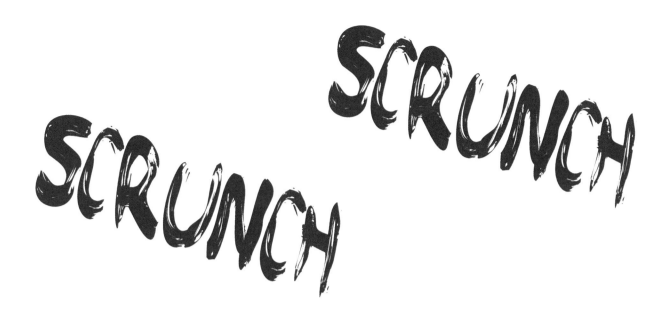

Sibley felt something under the covers.
She started to scream and then laughed.
The intruder was Sibley's cat, Stanley.
He was under the covers in
a teeny-weeny space beside her.

"I'm okay.
I'm okay.
Are you okay?"
Sibley asked.

"Meow," Stanley said
as he snuggled closer.

Sibley felt a little better.

But there were still
jiggly,
wiggly,
and
squiggly feelings
in her belly.

GURGLE
GURGLE
GLUMP!

The pipes in the walls of
the old house rattled.
Sibley and Stanley jumped
so high they almost
fell off the bed.
They looked at each other.

"I'm okay.
You're okay.
Are we okay?"
Sibley asked.

"Meow,"
Stanley said.
But Sibley did not feel okay.

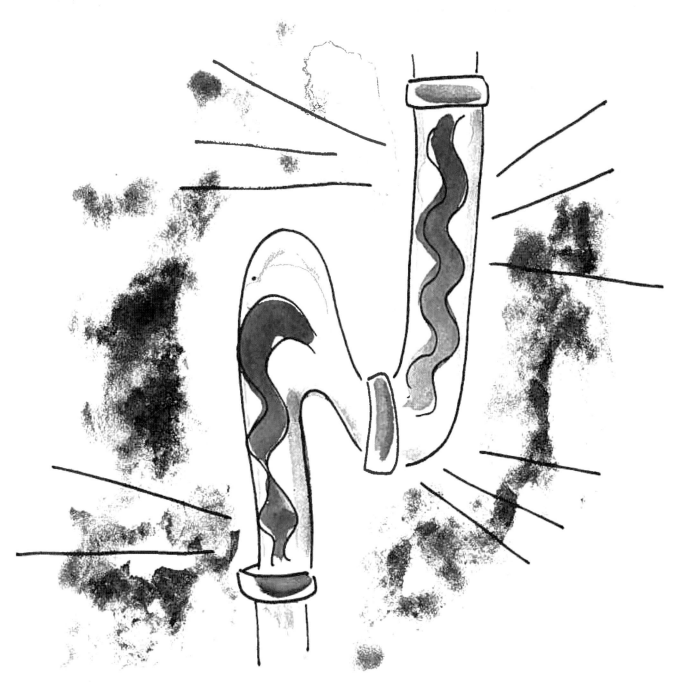

It was dark and she was scared.
She did not like strange noises.
She felt jiggly,
wiggly, and
squiggly
in her belly.

PITTER PATTER PITTER PATTER

Sibley and Stanley heard the rain
fall on the roof above their heads.

The pipes went
gurgle, gurgle, glump,
and the rain went
pitter patter, pitter patter.

This time they didn't jump.

"I'm okay.
You're okay.
Are we okay?"
Sibley asked.

"Meow," Stanley said.

Sibley hugged Stanley.

She did not feel as
jiggly, wiggly,
or squiggly
in her belly.

KAWOMP! KAWOMP!

Sibley's bedroom door flew wide open.
Sibley didn't jump. She knew that sound.
It was Snoozer, Sibley's big, fluffy, puffy,
scruffy puppy. He flew into the room.
He was afraid of the rain.

The pipes went gurgle, gurgle, glump.
The rain went pitter patter, pitter patter.
The door went kawomp, kawomp
as it swung back and forth.

"I'm okay.
You're okay,"
Sibley said to Stanley.

"Meow," Stanley said.

"I'm okay.
Are you okay?"
Sibley asked Snoozer.

Snoozer was so scared, he was shaking.
"Ruff, ruff," he said and
climbed onto the bed.

Sibley let out a long, slow
breath and hugged her friends.

She felt less
jiggly, wiggly,
and squiggly
in her belly.

Sibley, Stanley and Snoozer heard
footsteps on the bedroom floor.
Creak, creak, creak.
Then they heard
gurgle, gurgle, glump,
pitter patter, pitter patter,
kawomp, kawomp.

Sibley, Stanley and Snoozer
looked at each other.
"What is that creaking sound?" Sibley asked.

"Meow," Stanley said.

"Ruff, ruff," Snoozer said.

Sibley's little brother, Sam,
pushed his head under her bed covers.

Sibley giggled.
"Come up, Sam," she said.
"I'm okay.
We're okay.
Are you okay?"

"Yawnnnn, yawnnnn."
Sam curled up and fell fast asleep.

Sibley sat in the dark.
She only felt a tiny bit
jiggly, wiggly,
and squiggly
in her belly.

Zzzzzz, Zzzzzz

Sam quietly snored.

Purrrrr, Purrrr

Stanley happily purred.

Ruuuffff, ruffff

Snoozer barked in his dreams.

The pipes went
gurgle, gurgle, glump

The rain went
pitter patter, pitter patter

The door went
kawomp, kawomp
and stopped.

Sibley did not feel
jiggly, wiggly,
or squiggly
in her belly.
She wasn't scared anymore.

Sibley lay down
in her comfy bed.

She
smiled
and
slowly
closed
her eyes.

"I'm okay.
You're okay.
We are all okay,"
she
whispered,
and
fell
fast
asleep.

About the Author

After decades of working in health care, Dr. Kimberly Brayman was inspired to build confidence, normalize struggle, inspire hope, and delight adults and children alike through her storytelling.

She believes stories build empathy and empower the listener to find their own self-reliance and strength. The power of supportive relationships is a strong theme in her stoties. When a child knows deep in their heart that they are loved and accepted, just the way they are, they have a chance to blossom.

Dr. Brayman also loves to create with almost anything she can find. In this book she has graced the pages with some of her whimsical watercolors.

As of 2021, she was a registered psychologist (registration #2464) in British Columbia, Canada.

Other Illustrated Children's Books by Dr. Kimberly Brayman

Artsy Alphabet
Count With Me!
Nana Loves You More
Blueberries
I Want to Be
We Are Different and the Same
Will You Be My Friend?
The Magical Fisherman

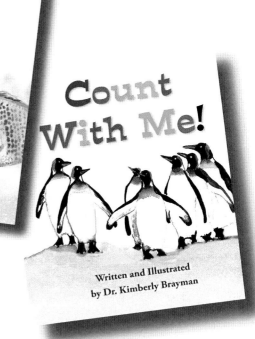

Available

on Amazon

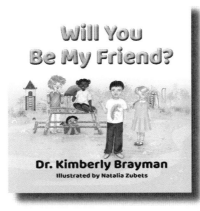

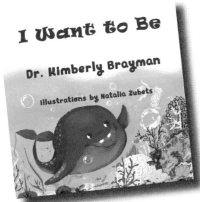

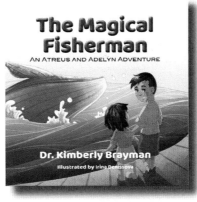

Chapter Books for Young Readers
Marshmallow the Magic Cat Adventures

Avry's Magical Cat: A Marshmallow the Magic Cat Adventure
Avry adopts a cat from the animal shelter and discovers he is magical like her Nana. She lives close to nature and has a magical view of the world. Available on Amazon.

A Troll in the Woods: A Marshmallow the Magic Cat Adventure
A true quest that shows courage and fear can go hand in hand, and the power of friendship to inspire action. Available on Amazon.

Avry and Atreus Save Christmas: A Marshmallow the Magic Cat Adventure
A delightful Christmas tale to be read every holiday season. It's full of elves, ravens, and the capability inside all children to redeem themselves and be good. Available on Amazon.

Marshmallow Paints the Town: A Marshmallow the Magic Cat Adventure
A fun story that focuses on collaboration, self-responsibility, making mistakes and recovering. Available on Amazon.

Marshmallow Gets a Little Sister: A Marshmallow the Magic Cat Adventure
Avry brings home a stray kitten, which makes Marshmallow very unhappy. He does not want a little sister and he wants to get rid of her. Is there really enough love to go around? On sale mid-2021.

Visit the author's website at KimberlyBraymanAuthor.com for updates.

Older children love the adventures of Marshmallow the Magic Cat

Get yours
now
on Amazon

Made in the USA
Monee, IL
07 June 2021